GRIMM'S
FAIRY TALES

This book belongs to

....

GRIMM'S
FAIRY TALES

Illustrated and retold
by Val Biro

AWARD PUBLICATIONS LIMITED

ISBN 978-1-84135-505-4

Copyright © Val Biro

First published 2008

Published by Award Publications Limited,
The Old Riding School, The Welbeck Estate,
Worksop, Nottinghamshire, S80 3LR

www.awardpublications.co.uk

1 3 5 7 9 10 8 6 4 2
08 10 12 14 16 18 20 19 17 15 13 11 09

Printed in Malaysia

CONTENTS

Snow White
and the
Seven Dwarfs

Once upon a winter's day, a Queen sat sewing at her open window. As she looked out at the snow that lay over the palace gardens, she pricked her finger with the needle, and three drops of blood fell on the snow, turning it rosy pink.

"How beautiful it looks," she thought.
And, in that moment, she wished for a child
with skin as white as snow, rosy pink cheeks
and hair as black as the ebony window frame.

Soon she had a daughter, with
skin as white as snow, rosy cheeks
and hair as black as ebony; and she
was called Snow White.

But sadly, the Queen died, and a
year later the King married again.

The new Queen was beautiful, but so vain that she could not bear anyone to be lovelier than herself. She would often look into her magic mirror and ask:

Mirror, mirror on the wall,
Who's the fairest of us all?
And the mirror would answer, "O Queen, you are the fairest in the land." Then she was pleased, because her mirror always spoke the truth.

But Snow White grew up, and by the age of seven she was lovelier than the Queen herself. This made the Queen so jealous, she could hardly bring herself to look at Snow White.

Instead, she looked at herself in the mirror and asked:
*Mirror, mirror on
the wall,
Who's the fairest
of us all?*

And the mirror replied:
O Queen, lovely
*   though you are,*
Snow White is
*   lovelier by far!*

This made her so angry that she told one of her servants to take Snow White into the wild wood and kill her. "I never want to see her again!" she told him.

The servant hurried away and, carrying
Snow White on his horse, he rode out of the
castle and across the hills, until they reached
the middle of the wild wood. There, he set her
down on the ground and pulled out his knife.

"Please don't hurt me!" sobbed Snow White. "I will run away and promise never to return!"

The servant felt sorry for the poor child and let her go. The wild beasts would soon make a meal of her anyway, he thought, and he was glad not to have to kill her himself.

So Snow White was left alone in the wild
wood. She was very frightened and began to
run, though she had no idea where she was
going. The wild beasts hiding in the trees saw
her distress and did not harm her.

It was almost dark when Snow White finally came across a little house in a clearing. Too tired to run any further, she knocked on the door – but there was no answer. Opening the door gently, Snow White stepped inside.

Everything in the house seemed neat and
tidy, but curiously small. There was a low table
laid with seven little plates and seven little
mugs. As Snow White was so hungry, she took
a little food and drink from each place in turn.

Then she saw seven little beds against the wall. One of them was a little larger than the others, and as Snow White was so very tired, she crawled into it, pulled up the covers and was soon fast asleep.

Before long, the owners
of the little house came home.
They were seven dwarfs, who
worked in the hills digging
for gold. As soon as they
went in, they realised
that someone had
been there.

"Hey! Someone's been tasting my food and
drink!" one of the dwarfs complained.
The others crowded round the table. "Yes!
Our food's been nibbled, too!" they cried.

The tallest dwarf looked around, and cried out suddenly. "Quick! Come and see! There's someone in my bed!"

They gathered round the bed, astonished to see a lovely child sleeping soundly there.

Careful not to wake her, the dwarfs ate their supper and went to their beds, making room for their brother so that they didn't disturb their visitor.

The next morning, Snow White was as surprised to see the seven little men as they had been to see her. She told them her sad story while they ate breakfast, and hoped that they would let her stay with them. The dwarfs talked it over among themselves.

"If you promise to keep our house neat and tidy, and cook our meals," said the first dwarf at last, "then you can stay."

"Oh, I will, I will!" said Snow White. "Thank you all so much!"

The good dwarfs all cheered.

And so it was. Every morning, the dwarfs left to work in the gold and copper mines in the hills, while Snow White remained at home to do all the housework.

The dwarfs grew very fond of her, and each
day warned her to look out for her stepmother.
"She is sure to find out where you are. So
don't let anyone in the house!"

But the wicked Queen still
thought Snow White was dead.
Then, one day she went to her
magic mirror and asked it
her usual
question.

This time the mirror replied:
You must know that Snow White lives
with seven dwarfs among the hills.
O Queen, you may be lovely too,
but she's far lovelier than you!
The Queen shook the mirror in her rage.

Determined now to deal with Snow White herself, the Queen masked her face, and disguised as an old pedlar-woman she set out into the wild wood to find the home of the seven dwarfs.

"Pretty necklaces!
Who will buy my
pretty necklaces?"
she croaked outside
Snow White's window.

The necklace sparkled
so prettily that Snow
White thought there
would be no harm in
taking a look.

"This one is just right for you, my dear," said
the old woman. "Come, let me put it on for you."
But she pulled it so tightly around Snow
White's throat, that the poor child choked and
fell down in a dead faint.

"There's an end to all your beauty!" snarled
the wicked Queen, leaving her for dead.

The seven dwarfs were horrified when they came home and saw Snow White sprawled on the ground. But then they saw the tight necklace round her neck and cut it loose at once. Snow White gasped for breath and in a little while sat up and began to feel better.

As soon as she was home again, the wicked Queen went straight to her mirror, but once again it said:

O Queen, you may be lovely too,
But Snow White is far lovelier than you!

The queen screamed in anger. "Still alive! Now I will find something that will definitely put an end to you!"

She took an apple that was golden on one side and red on the other, and filled the red side with poison. Then she disguised herself as a farmer's wife, put the apple carefully in a basket with some others, and set off once more for the house of the seven dwarfs.

"Sweet apples for sale! Lovely, juicy apples!" she called out as she reached the house.

Snow White opened the window. "I'm not allowed to let anyone in," she said.

"Won't you just try one?" said the woman. But Snow White shook her head.

"Are you afraid it's poisoned?" asked the woman, and she cut the apple in half. "Here, you have the lovely red half and I'll eat the other."

But as soon as Snow White bit into the poisoned apple, she fell senseless to the ground.

The queen cackled with
glee as she went on her way.
Fortunately, the seven dwarfs came
home early that day. When they lifted
Snow White from the ground, the
poisoned apple fell from her mouth and
she was saved. The dwarfs reminded her
that she must be even more careful, for
the wicked Queen might yet come again.

Back at her castle, the Queen put on all her finest clothes before she went to look in her mirror. But when she heard exactly the same answer as before, she cried, "Snow White shall die, if it costs me my life!" and rushed out.

She went straight to her secret witch's den, and there she brewed a terrible potion, into which she dipped a golden comb.

Putting on yet another disguise, she returned to the house of the seven dwarfs.

When Snow White heard a knock at the door, she opened the window and saw an old beggar selling combs.

Forgetting the dwarfs' warning, she felt so sorry for the old man that she bought the comb he offered to her.

But as soon as she fixed the comb into her ebony hair, the potion worked its magic and Snow White fell down, dead.

"This time the dwarfs won't be able to wake you up again!" sneered the beggar, who was, of course, the wicked Queen in disguise.

Back home in her castle, the Queen went straight to her mirror.

Mirror, mirror on the wall,
Who is the fairest of us all?
And the mirror at last replied:
O Queen, you are the fairest
in the land.

And the wicked Queen was happy, as far as a wicked heart can ever be.

The dwarfs came home to find Snow White lying upon the ground, and nothing they did could revive her. They laid her gently on a bed and wept.

This time, Snow White was truly dead.

"We cannot bury her in the cold earth," they said. So they put her in a glass coffin instead, and on it they mounted a plaque, engraved with her name and that she was a king's daughter. They placed the coffin on a mound sheltered by trees.

The dwarfs took it in turn to watch over her. The birds and the creatures of the forest came too, and all mourned Snow White.

And so she remained for a long, long time, and still she looked as lovely as ever – with skin as white as snow, rosy cheeks and hair as black as ebony – as if she were only sleeping.

It happened one day that a Prince came riding through the wild wood and saw the coffin. As soon as he gazed upon Snow White – who had by then grown into a beautiful young lady – he fell deeply in love with her.

"I cannot live without her!" he said. "Please let me take her with me," he begged the dwarfs.

"Not for all the gold in the world!" was their reply. But the Prince was so heartbroken that eventually they agreed to let him take Snow White and the coffin back to his castle.

The moment he lifted it up, the poisoned
comb fell out of Snow White's hair and she
opened her eyes. "Where am I?" she asked.

"You are with me," said the Prince. "I love
you more than all the world, and I want you to
be my wife."

The happy news of the Prince's engagement spread throughout the land. The seven dwarfs were, of course, invited to the royal wedding, but the wicked Queen was not.

The next time that she went to her mirror, she asked:

Mirror, mirror tell me true,
Who's the fairest, tell me who?

The mirror answered:

O Queen, lovely though you are,
The new Princess is lovelier by far!

The Queen cried out bitterly, "Who is this new Princess? How dare she be lovelier than me?" She put on her grandest clothes and went to the Prince's palace to see the Princess for herself.

Imagine her startled surprise when
she arrived and saw that the Princess was
none other than Snow White! The Queen
gave a strangled cry and fainted clean away.

Her footmen carried the wicked Queen back
to her coach and returned her to the castle.

And there she remained for the rest of her
days, growing old and ugly.

But Snow White and her Prince lived for
many years in peace and happiness.

The Bremen Town Musicians

There was once a donkey who worked for a miller, carrying sacks of flour to market. But the work was heavy and the donkey was not as strong as he used to be. It was time for him to leave the mill and look for lighter work.

"I've always had a fine voice," he said to himself. "Maybe I can get a job as a musician."

He liked the idea, and set out cheerfully for the city of Bremen.

On the way, he saw a dog lying by the side of the road, looking miserable.

"What's wrong, my friend?" asked the donkey.

"My master has turned me out," howled the dog. "He says I'm no good at hunting. How will I earn a living now?"

"I'm off to Bremen, to be a musician," said the donkey. "Why don't you come too? You've got a strong voice. We could sing duets."

"What a good idea," said the dog, cheering up. "Yes, I'll come with you."

So they jogged on along the road together.

They had not gone far
when they saw a cat squatting in
the middle of the road, looking glum.
"What's up with you?" asked the
donkey. The cat mewed miserably.
"My mistress said that as I'm useless at
catching mice, she will put me down. I didn't
like the sound of that, so I ran away."

"Just as well you did," said the donkey. "You have a fine voice, so why don't you come with us to Bremen and become a musician? You can be our lead singer."

The cat liked the sound of that very much, so she stretched herself and joined the others.

Not far down the road, the three animals passed a farm. A rooster was perched on the gatepost. "Cock-a-doodle-do!" he crowed, making them jump.

"What's the matter with you?" asked the donkey.

"It's the farmer's wife," the rooster explained. "She wants to chop off my head and cook me in a soup!"

"That won't do at all," said the donkey.
"Come with us to Bremen instead and become
a town musician. Far better than becoming
chicken soup!"

"I should say so," said the rooster, and he
flew down from the gatepost and joined them.

The four animals went
cheerfully on their way,
until they reached a forest.

By then it was getting dark, so they decided
to spend the night there. Each of them chose
somewhere to sleep: the dog and the donkey lay
under a tree, the cat settled on a branch above
and the rooster flew to one on the other side.

From his perch, the rooster noticed a light
twinkling in the distance. "I can see a light
over there. Shall we go and see what it is?"
The others felt hungry, so they willingly
agreed, hoping they might find some dinner.

It was a house. And as the musicians crept towards the window, the donkey – being the tallest – looked in.

"What can you see?" asked the rooster.

"I can see a table laden with wonderful food – but there's a gang of robbers eating it all up!"

"Never mind them," barked the dog. "I'm hungry!"

"Me, too," miaowed the cat. "But how shall we get in?"

That was a good question. They talked
about it for a while, until they had a plan.

They went back to
the window.

The donkey put his
forefeet on the sill, the
dog jumped onto his
back, the cat stood on
the dog and the rooster
perched on the cat's
head. Then the donkey
tapped a foot and the
four musicians began
to sing at the top of
their voices. There
never was such a din!

Then they all crashed through the window, braying, howling, mewing and crowing wildly, frightening the robbers into a panic.

They were sure that a howling
demon had broken in, so they tumbled out
of the door and fled, terrified, into the forest.

Now that the musicians
had the house to themselves,
they settled round the table
to finish the meal that the
robbers had left.

It was delicious!

After their meal, the weary band blew out the candles and each animal found somewhere to sleep.

The cat curled up by the fire.

The dog slept by the door.

The donkey dozed outside in the yard, and the rooster perched up on the roof.

Later that night one of the robbers crept
back to the house to see if the demons had gone.
He went to light the candle in the embers of
the fire…

…and the cat hissed
and scratched his face!
Terrified, he ran to
the door…

…where the dog leapt up and bit him on the leg!

The robber fled across the yard, where the donkey gave him a painful kick. His cries woke the rooster, who went *cock-a-doodle-doo* noisily from the roof.

Shaking with fright, the robber ran back to the rest of the gang.

"It's terrible back there!" he wailed. "The house is full of fiends!

"I went to light the candle, but a spitting witch nearly scratched my eyes out!

"So I ran to the door, but some snarling creature stabbed me in the leg!

"When I ran into the yard, a fearful monster beat me with a club.

"And then there's that judge who screamed 'Lock him in the loo!'

"I was lucky to get out of there alive!"

The robbers didn't dare return to the house ever again.

But the Bremen Town Musicians liked it so much they decided to stay, and their music became famous for miles around.

So they had no need to visit Bremen after all.

The Golden Goose

There was once a man who had three sons, called Harry, Sam and Billy.

The first two were clever young men, so people called them Handyharry and Smartysam.

But Billy wasn't too bright, so they called him Sillybilly.

One day, Handyharry went off to
the forest to cut wood. His mother
gave him a sweet pancake and a
bottle of wine for his lunch.

When he got to the forest…

…he met a little old man with a long grey beard.

"Good morning," said Greybeard. "Could you please spare me a little food and drink? I am so hungry and thirsty."

"Certainly not," said Handyharry. "I only have enough for myself. Be off with you!"

And he went on his way to cut wood.

But as he was working, his axe slipped and cut his leg.

Handyharry cursed and leapt about in pain, and then headed for home, limping all the way.

Little did he know that it was no accident.

When his brother arrived home without
any wood, Smartysam went off to the forest.
He also took a pancake and wine with him.

In the forest, he too met the same little old
man who asked him for some food and drink.

"If I give you my lunch, I won't have enough
for myself," said Smartysam. "Be off with you!"

Shortly, he began to chop wood. But before long, his axe slipped, too, and cut his foot.

To be sure, this was no accident, either.

Smartysam had to borrow a donkey to carry him home.

With both of his brothers unable to work,
it was up to Sillybilly to go and chop wood.
But his mother only gave him a stale pancake
and sour beer to take with him.

In the forest, he too met Greybeard.

"Could you spare me something to eat and
drink?" asked the little old man. "I am so very
hungry and thirsty."

"Certainly," said Sillybilly. "As long as you
don't mind stale pancake and sour beer."

So they sat down together to eat. But when Sillybilly tasted his pancake, it was fresh and delicious, and the sour beer had become fine wine.

When they had finished, Greybeard smiled, and said, "As you have such a good heart and were so willing to share your lunch, I shall give you good luck. Cut down that old tree and you'll find something amongst the roots."

And with that, the little man disappeared.

Sillybilly cut down the tree,
as Greybeard had told him, and
there amongst the roots in the
hollow trunk, he found a goose!

But it was no ordinary goose.
Its feathers were pure gold.

It was getting late. Sillybilly picked up the goose and went to stay at an inn for the night.

Now, the innkeeper's three daughters spotted the goose and were amazed. How they would love some of its golden feathers!

Early the next morning, Sillybilly left the inn with the golden goose. He didn't notice the three sisters following him.

One of the girls reached out to pluck a feather from the goose – but her hand got stuck to it!

The second girl tried to push her sister aside, but got her hand stuck to her sister's dress!

And when the third girl tried to tug the second back, her hand got stuck to her sister's apron strings!

So the three girls had to run behind Sillybilly – willy-nilly!

Now, a parson walking by saw the girls and cried, "For shame!" and seized the youngest by the hand – and got stuck fast.

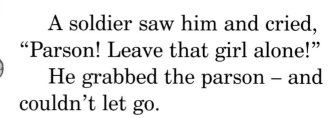

A soldier saw him and cried, "Parson! Leave that girl alone!" He grabbed the parson – and couldn't let go.

A clerk saw him and
cried, "Soldier! Don't hurt
His Reverence!" He caught hold
of him – and got stuck
in his turn.

Then a farmer rushed up to
pull the clerk free – and got
stuck as well!

So there were seven of them trailing behind
Sillybilly and his goose, as they reached a town.

Now, the mayor of the town was very rich and had a pretty daughter called Milly. Sadly, Milly had never learned how to laugh or even smile. Nothing that anyone could do seemed to help. Desperate to see his daughter happy, the mayor announced that whoever could make her laugh could marry her.

When Sillybilly saw the proclamation posted by the town gate, he could not resist trying his luck. Clutching his goose, he went to the Town Hall.

Of course, what Sillybilly, didn't realise
was that the three sisters, the parson, the
soldier, the clerk and the farmer went too.

As it happened, the mayor and his daughter were on the balcony. When they saw the young man cradling a goose, with seven people cavorting and tumbling behind him, Milly began to laugh. And laugh… and laugh. It was as if she would never stop!

At the sound of Milly's laughter, Sillybilly stopped and turned to look at her.

Immediately, the sticky magic spell was broken. The parson, the soldier, the clerk, the farmer and the three silly sisters all came unstuck and fell about, exhausted.

Sillybilly ran upstairs to the balcony – goose and all – and asked Milly to marry him.

But the mayor didn't want a sillybilly for a son-in-law.

"You can marry her on one condition," he said. "You must bring me a ship that can sail on land and water!"

It was impossible! Wasn't it?

At once, Sillybilly thought of his friend,
Greybeard. Quickly, he ran back through the
forest until he found the little old man and
explained his problem.

"Since you were so kind to me," said
Greybeard, "I'll be glad to help. Come!"

Greybeard led Sillybilly down to the river,
and there was a magnificent ship, with her sails
set and smoke puffing out of her funnel.

Sillybilly sailed the ship into the town harbour, and there the ship came out of the water and steamed up the jetty on her great iron wheels.

"Here's the ship, my Lord Mayor!" Sillybilly cried. "Now may I marry your daughter?"

The mayor was amazed at the wonderful craft, and realized the young man was not so silly after all.

"Yes," he said at last. "You may marry Milly, Billy."

Milly giggled, and everyone laughed and cheered.

After the wedding, the happy couple sailed away together in the wonderful ship, on their honeymoon.

And of course, the golden goose went with them too.

The Elves and
the Shoemaker

There was once a good shoemaker, who had become poor because business was so bad. Soon he had no materials left but just enough leather to make one last pair of shoes.

So one night he cut the shoes out, intending to make them the next day, and went to bed.

In the morning, however, when the shoemaker went to start work, he was amazed to find the shoes standing on his table, completely finished. They were perfectly made, with every stitch neatly in place, as if they had come from a master. The shoemaker did not know what to think.

Just then, an important-looking customer came into the shop.

"What a handsome pair of shoes!" he exclaimed, as he tried them on. They fitted perfectly, so he bought them straight away, and was so pleased with them that he paid double the usual price.

The shoemaker used the money to buy more leather, and that night, before bedtime, he cut out two pairs of shoes. The next morning – wonder of wonders! – two pairs of beautifully-made shoes stood ready on his table; and people were already at the door, eager to buy them.

And so it went on, night after night: what he had cut out in the evening was finished by next morning, each pair of shoes more perfect than the last.

News of the wonderful shoes went round the town, and crowds of people came to queue outside the shop to buy them.

Business was certainly looking up, and eventually the shoemaker became quite wealthy.

One night, the shoemaker and his wife decided to stay up to see who was helping them so generously. So they lit a candle and hid behind the door to watch.

On the stroke of midnight, two little elves, dressed in rags, appeared in the room and settled down on the worktable. They began to thread and sew, tap and hammer so nimbly that the shoemaker could barely believe his eyes. They did not stop until all the shoes were ready and left standing on the table.

Then, the two elves disappeared.

The next morning the wife said, "Those elves have made us rich. Let us show them how grateful we are. They must be cold in those rags, so I tell you what I'll do. I shall make them some smart warm clothes to wear."

The shoemaker agreed and said that for his part he would make them shoes and hats. So they sat down and worked hard all day.

When they had finished everything – the little shirts, waistcoats, jackets, trousers, stockings, shoes and hats – they laid them out on the table and hid themselves, to wait for the elves.

On the stroke of midnight, the two little elves came bounding in, ready to work.

But instead of the cut-out leather, they saw the smart little clothes laid out on the table.

At first they were astonished, but when they realised that these were presents from the shoemaker, the elves got dressed quickly, and began to dance and skip all around the table, for sheer joy.

Then they burst into song:

Now we are so
smartly dressed,
We'll give the cobbling
work a rest!

And so singing, they danced right out of the
front door.

From that time on, the elves came no more. But the shoemaker's shoes had become famous, and people flocked from far and wide to buy them, and he and his wife were never poor again.

The Wolf
and the
Seven Little Kids

Once upon a time there was a Mother Goat who had seven little kids. She loved them all dearly, and cared for them well.

But one day, she decided to leave them at home while she went to the shops. Before she went, she reminded them all to be very careful.

"Beware of that wicked wolf!" she told them. "Don't let him in, whatever you do. You'll know him by his gruff voice and big black feet."

"We'll be careful, Maaa," said the seven little kids.

Now, not long after their mother
had left, there was a knock on the
cottage door.

"I'm home, children!"
said a gruff voice.

"Open the door –
I have a present
for you all."

"You are not our mother,"
said the kids. "She has a sweet
soft voice, but yours is gruff.
You're the wolf! Go away!"

So the wolf went off to a shop and bought a large lump of chalk, which he ate to make his voice softer.

Then he crept back to Goat Cottage.

Crouching under the
window, he called softly:
"I'm back, children!
And I've bought a
present for each
one of you!"

But the seven little kids saw his big black
foot on the windowsill.
"You're the wolf! Go away!"

The wolf ran off to the
baker's shop.

"I've hurt my paw," he said.
"Put some dough on it for me."

The baker was too nervous of
the wolf to refuse, and he did as he
was told.

Next, the wolf ran off
to the miller.

"Put some flour on this paw of
mine," he growled.

The miller was too scared of the wolf to
say no, so he put the flour on.

The wolf returned
to Goat Cottage and
knocked on the door
again.

"Open the door,
children!" he called.
"It's me – your mother!"

The seven little kids heard the soft voice,
and saw the white paw he showed them.
So they believed him and opened the door.

But it was the wolf, of course. And he burst into the room, huge and horrible.

The seven terrified kids hid themselves wherever they could.

The first hid under the table,

the second in the bed,

the third in the laundry basket,

the fourth behind the chair,

the fifth in
the cupboard,

the sixth
behind the
sofa,

and the
seventh in the
clock case.

But the wolf found them
all, and one by one swallowed
them down.

All except the youngest,
hiding in the clock case.

After such an enormous meal, the wolf
tottered out out of the cottage and lay under a
tree to sleep.

When mother goat came home, what a sorry sight met her eyes! The house was wrecked and her children were gone.

All except the youngest, who had been hiding in the clock.

"Maaa! Maaa!" she cried. "It was the wolf!"
And she told her mother all that had happened.

They rushed outside and found the wolf still fast asleep, and snoring under the tree.

"Look, Maaa!" said the little kid.

"His huge tummy is moving!"

"Quick!" whispered mother goat. "Fetch me the large scissors, and a needle and thread. Hurry! Before he wakes up!"

Snip, *snip*, went the scissors and
– yes! – out jumped her kids from
the wolf's tummy. They were quite
unharmed, because the greedy
wolf had swallowed
them whole.

Mother Goat was overjoyed to see her kids
again, but she had one more thing to do.

"Run and fetch me some big stones from the riverbank," she told the kids. "We shall fill the wolf's tummy with them."

And that's exactly what they did. Mother Goat then sewed up the wolf's tummy so quickly and cleverly, that the wolf slept through it all.

When the wolf woke up at last, he was thirsty.
As he got to his feet, the stones in his
stomach knocked and rattled against each other,
and he groaned:

There is something rather
funny,
Going on inside my tummy.
Instead of those sweet kids
I ate –
It feels like rocks. Oh, what
a weight!

He staggered down to the river and bent
forward to have a drink – but the heavy stones
in his stomach made him lose his balance and...

Splash!

The wolf fell head first into the river and was swept away, never to be seen again.

The Magic Porridge Pot

Once there was a poor little girl, called Lotte, who lived with her mother in a small cottage at the top end of the village.

They were so very poor that one day they had nothing at all left to eat.

"Go into the forest, Lotte," said her mother,
"and try to find us some berries."

Lotte went, but she couldn't find any. She
felt cold and hungry, and began to cry.

"Don't cry, little girl," came a kindly voice.

Lotte looked up and saw an old
woman standing in front of her.
"I know all about your
troubles," said the kindly
witch-woman, "and as
you are a good girl,
I'll give you this."
She held out a
small iron pot.

"When you are hungry, just say '*Cook, little pot, cook,*' and it will make good, sweet porridge. And when you say '*Stop little pot, now!*' it will stop cooking."

Saying this, the woman smiled at Lotte and then disappeared.

When she got home, Lotte put the pot on
the table and said, "*Cook, little pot, cook,*" and
– to her mother's amazement – the little iron
pot filled to the brim with bubbling, delicious
sweet porridge!

Then Lotte said, "*Stop little pot, now!*"

The pot stopped cooking, and they both had
a wonderful meal.

From that day on, Lotte and her mother ate porridge whenever they liked.

One day, when Lotte went to play with her friends at the other end of the village, her mother wanted some lunch.

"*Cook, little pot, cook,*" she ordered, and the pot began cooking; and after she had eaten enough, she wanted it to stop.

But she had forgotten the right words! So the pot went on cooking and the porridge ran over the table.

It filled first the kitchen and then the whole house. It burst out through the door and windows and Lotte's mother leapt into a tree to escape. But still she couldn't remember how to stop the pot.

The bubbling porridge flowed on to fill the next house and then the whole street. But the little pot continued to cook, just as if it wanted to feed the whole world.

People tried desperately to save themselves from the gooey flood, and they climbed onto roofs and up the church tower, as the village was engulfed by the tide of porridge.

Soon there was only one house left, where Lotte was playing. She guessed at once what must have happened, and at the top of her voice she shouted, "*STOP LITTLE POT, NOW!*" And the pot stopped cooking at once.

After that, the villagers had to eat their way back to their homes.

To eat the village clean took them all winter!

Mind you, the magic porridge tasted just as delicious, even cold.

Lucky Hans

After working for his master for seven years, young Hans decided it was time to leave. "I'd like to go and see my mother," he explained, "and to seek my fortune elsewhere."

"You've worked hard," said his master, "and deserve to be well rewarded. Here, take this." And he gave Hans a gold nugget as big as his head. "Good Luck!"

Hans thanked him and set off for home.

As he stumbled along with the heavy nugget on his shoulder, he met a rider trotting along on a fine-looking horse.

"Oh," said Hans aloud. "How I wish I could ride too, and sit in comfort. I'd save on shoe leather as well!"

"So why are you walking, then?" asked the man.

"I must," said Hans, "for I have this nugget to carry home. Sure, it's gold, but it's so very heavy."

"I'll tell you what," said the man, "let's exchange your nugget for my horse."

"Gladly!" cried Hans, handing over the gold and scrambling onto the horse. He was delighted with the bargain…

…and so was the man, who promptly ran off with the nugget.

It was blissful to be free of his burden.

"How lucky I am!" thought Hans, cheerfully. "Giddyup, horse!"

The horse broke into a brisk canter...

...and before he knew it, Hans was flying through the air and into the roadside ditch.

As it happened, a farmer was just passing, taking a cow to market. He caught the horse while Hans climbed out of the ditch.

"Riding is a fool's game," complained Hans. "I'm never getting on that horse again!"

But he cheered up when he saw the cow. "Now that's a different matter! You can walk quietly behind a cow; and what's more, you can have milk and butter and cheese at any time you wish!"

"Well, then," said the farmer. "To give you that pleasure, I am prepared to exchange my cow for your horse."

Hans was delighted with the bargain and thought again how lucky he was. What more could he possibly need?

The farmer, meanwhile, jumped onto the horse and galloped away.

As Hans headed towards home with the cow, he became hungry. So he sat down in the shade of a tree and ate up all the food he had brought – lunch, supper and all – while his cow grazed contentedly beside him.

"Life is really good," thought Hans.

The day was hot and as he continued on his journey, Hans became thirsty. But he had nothing to drink.

Then he laughed. "Look! A bucket of milk is walking right in front of me!" He had no bucket, though, so he put his leather hat under the cow to milk her.

But no milk would come out.

Hans was so
clumsy at milking that
the cow lost her patience and
gave him such a kick that Hans
went flying through the air and landed,
senseless, flat on his back. He only came to
when he heard someone call out.

It was a butcher who happened to come that way, pushing a wheelbarrow with a pig in it. He gave Hans a drink from his flask, while Hans told him what had happened.

"Someone has played a trick on you," said the butcher.

"This cow won't give you milk any more, because she's too old. She is only fit for the butcher now."

Hans scratched his head. "So I've been cheated! I don't like beef much, anyway. That pig of yours would be much better: think of all the tasty ham and sausages!"

"Listen, Hans," said the butcher, "I'd like to do you a personal favour, as a friend, and let you have my pig in exchange for your cow."

"Oh, thank you!" said Hans, as he handed over the cow. How lucky he was! When things went wrong, they turned out right every time! Hans went cheerfully on his way, pushing the pig in the barrow.

Presently he met a boy carrying a fat turkey. "That'll make a fine feast for someone," said Hans. "It's nearly as good as my pig."

"I know," said the boy, looking around furtively. "But listen. Somebody stole a pig in that village and took it away in a barrow. I'm pretty sure that this is the same pig. If you're caught, they'll send you to prison."

Hans was horrified. "Goodness! Help me out of this! You know your way around here; take my pig and leave me the turkey," he begged.

"It's risky," said the boy, "but I can't let you get into trouble." So he took the barrow and wheeled the pig quickly away.

Hans was greatly relieved, as he tucked the turkey under his arm. "And how pleased mother will be with this fine bird!"

As he arrived in the next village, he saw a knife-grinder, singing merrily as he worked:

I sharpen scissors and
  grind the blade,
And think of all the
  money I've made.

When the man saw Hans, he stopped his song and asked, "Tell me, where did you buy that fine turkey?"

"I didn't buy it. I
exchanged it for my pig."
"And the pig?"
"That I got for a cow."
"And the cow?"
"In exchange for a horse."
"And the horse?"
"For a gold nugget as big
as my head."
"And the gold?"
"It was my wages."

"Well," said the man, "you certainly know how to look after yourself. Just make sure that you always have money jingling in your pockets, as I have."

"How shall I manage that?" asked Hans.

"Simple. Become a knife-grinder like me! Look, here's my spare grindstone. I don't want anything for it except your turkey."

"What a bargain," thought Hans as he gladly exchanged his turkey for the stone. "I'll be rich!"

So he picked up the heavy stone and went on his way.

But the road went uphill and Hans was tired after such a long day. He thought how nice it would be not to have such a heavy stone to carry.

When at last he reached the top, Hans was so exhausted that he stumbled and dropped the stone. Down the hill it rolled, faster and faster, until it went flying over the edge and into a deep river, where it sank without trace.

Hans jumped up, joyfully. The nasty, heavy stone had gone!

"No one under the sun is as lucky as I am!" he laughed. And with a light heart and empty-handed, he danced and ran down the road towards home.

Hansel and Gretel

Once upon a time, there was a poor woodcutter who lived in a cottage at the edge of a big forest. He had two children whom he loved very much: a boy called Hansel and a girl called Gretel. Sadly, their mother had died when they were very young.

He had a new wife now, but she did not love
the children at all. She complained that they
ate so much that there was not enough food for
them all. Times were hard.

One night, she told her husband, "We shall starve if this goes on. We must take the children into the forest and leave them there – far enough so that they won't find their way back."

The woodcutter protested, but he could not argue with his wife, so he reluctantly agreed to her plan.

The children had heard them talking, and
Gretel began to cry. But Hansel hushed her and
said that he would think of something.

He slipped quietly out of the back door, and
when he saw a pile of white pebbles glinting in
the moonlight, he had an idea. He filled his
pockets with them and went back to bed.

The next morning, they all set out into the forest to cut wood. As their stepmother led them deeper and deeper into the forest, Hansel followed behind, secretly dropping the white pebbles, one by one, as he went.

"Now, children," said their stepmother when they stopped at last, "wait for us here while your father and I go and cut some wood. I shall call you when we are ready to leave."

The children waited and waited, but still their stepmother did not call them. And it was getting dark.

"They've left us!" sobbed Gretel, "and I am so cold and hungry."

"Don't worry, Gretel," said Hansel. "Come along, let's find the way home."

He wrapped his coat around her shoulders
as they set out for home. Soon it grew too dark
to see, until the moon came out from behind
the clouds. Then the children saw something
glinting on the ground.

"Look!" cried Hansel. "It's one of my white
pebbles! And there's another!"

The pebbles that Hansel had dropped on the way into the forest were now showing them the way out of it. How delighted the woodcutter was to see his children safely home again!

But times grew even
harder than before. So one
night, with only half a loaf
of bread left in the larder, the
stepmother took her husband into the
back yard and whispered, "This time we
must take the children into the forest
and make sure they never come back."

The woodcutter tried to protest again,
but she hissed, "No arguments!" and she
locked the back door from the outside.

The children heard everything, but this time
Hansel could not get at the white pebbles.
What were they going to do?

Early the next morning, their stepmother
gave the children each a slice of bread. Then
once again she led them all into the forest, to
a part where they had never been before.

Hansel had no pebbles, only his slice of
bread. So he dropped it, crumb by crumb, to
mark the way they had come. Soon there was
nothing left for him to eat.

In the very depths of the
forest, the stepmother once
again told the children to wait
until she came to fetch them.

But she did not return. Anxious to get home before it grew too dark, Hansel and Gretel set out to find the breadcrumbs which would show them the way.

But they couldn't find any – not a single one. The birds of the forest had eaten them all!

"Don't worry, " said Hansel. "We'll soon find
the way." But all night they stumbled this way
and that until they were too tired to go any
further. They were far from home and
completely lost.

As dawn broke, they woke cold and hungry. They saw a white bird sitting in the tree above them. It flew off a little way and stopped to look back at them. "It wants us to follow it," said Hansel. "Come on, Gretel."

The bird led them to a clearing, where it settled on the chimney of a small house that stood there. The two children ran towards it joyfully.

And what a wonderful house it was, entirely made of gingerbread, cakes and barley sugar! Delighted, the hungry children broke off pieces and crammed them into their mouths.

"Well, well, well!" croaked
an old woman from the doorway,
making the children jump. "So, you
like my gingerbread house. Come inside, both
of you, and I'll cook you a proper meal."

She was as good as her word and soon Hansel and Gretel were tucking into the best meal they had eaten for a long time, with second helpings as well.

Afterwards, the old woman showed them two little beds. Very full and tired, the children were soon fast asleep.

Now, you probably realise that this old
woman was, in fact, a witch. A very evil
witch, too, who used to tempt children
to visit her gingerbread house.
And once they had fattened up
nicely on her cooking, she
would cook them in the
oven for herself!

Sure enough, the next morning she seized
Hansel and locked him in a cage, and put
Gretel to work. "We must fatten the boy up,"
she cackled, as she gave him a huge bowl
of porridge.

Day after day she cooked big meals for both children, and every night she told Hansel to poke his finger out of the cage to see how fat he was getting.

Each time, Hansel poked a chicken bone out of the cage instead, and the witch – who was very short-sighted – thought he wasn't getting any fatter.

After a while, the witch lost all patience. "Fat or thin, I shall cook him now! Stoke up the oven, girl!" she commanded.

"Now then, my dear," she said more calmly, "have a look in the oven and see how hot it is."

Gretel knew that the witch meant to shut
the oven door behind her and cook her as well,
so she pretended not to understand.

"I don't know how to," she said.
"Could you show me?"

"You silly goose, it's easy," snapped the witch. "Like this!"

But she turned so abruptly that she tripped and lost her balance. With a horrible cry, the witch fell headlong into the flames.

Then the oven door swung to and slammed shut. *Bang!*

And that was the end of the wicked witch.

It only took Gretel a moment to open Hansel's cage, and he leapt out and embraced his sister. "Quick!" said Gretel. "We must get away before it gets dark."

They went outside and broke off as many pieces of gingerbread from the house as they could stuff into their pockets.

Then they saw the same white bird,
who seemed to be waiting for them.
Gratefully, the children followed as it
led them through the forest.

As darkness fell, though, the bird disappeared into its nest, leaving Hansel and Gretel on their own once more.

For a while, the children continued on their way, until it was too dark to see between the trees. They were hopelessly lost.

Just then, the moon rose above the clouds and something wonderful happened.

"Look!" whispered Gretel. There, on the ground in front of her, something glinted in the moonlight.

"It's one of my pebbles!" cried Hansel. "And look – there's another!" They had found the old path. Joyfully, the children began to run.

They ran and they ran, following the trail of pebbles until, at long last, they saw their home beyond the trees – and their dear father.

How they rejoiced and hugged each other!

The woodcutter had never forgiven himself for abandoning his children in the forest, and his wife had left him soon after. But now, with his children returned, he worked even harder than before and life began to get better.

With all their troubles over, Hansel and Gretel and their father were happy at last.